Tiny FoX and Great Boar

Dawn

Berenika Kołomycka

Tiny Fox and Great Boar

Dawn

Written and Illustrated by Berenika Kołomycka
Lettered by Crank!

AN ONI PRESS PUBLICATION

Designed by Kate Z. Stone and Sarah Rockwell
Edited by Grace Scheipeter

Published by Oni-Lion Forge Publishing Group, LLC.

Troy Look, vp of publishing services • Katie Sainz, director of marketing • Angie Knowles, director of design & production • Sarah Rockwell, senior graphic designer • Carey Soucy, senior graphic designer • Chris Cerasi, managing editor • Bess Pallares, senior editor Grace Scheipeter, senior editor • Gabriel Granillo, editor • Desiree Rodriguez, editor Zack Soto, editor • Ben Eisner, game developer • Sara Harding, executive assistant Jung Hu Lee, logistics coordinator • Kuian Kellum, warehouse assistant

Joe Nozemack, publisher emeritus

1319 SE Martin Luther King Jr. Blvd.
Suite 240
Portland, OR 97214

onipress.com
[f] [y] [@] @onipress

@berenikamess
@ccrank

First Edition: April 2023
ISBN: 978-1-63715-205-8
eISBN: 978-1-63715-923-1

1 2 3 4 5 6 7 8 9 10

Library of Congress Control Number: 2022940497

Printed in China

Day

It was a beautiful forest, full of tall trees.

The path Tiny Fox and Great Boar chose wound between fern fields and moss-covered rocks.

The sun was shining, and the air was pleasantly warm.
It is terribly lonely here.
Not really, Fox. We are in the wetlands. If you look carefully, you will see how many creatures live in these mosses and pools. See for yourself!

The small nymph climbed onto a leaf to better see the new visitors.

MBDL stands for the Most Beautiful Day in Life. It is when I will transform into a beautiful mayfly!

I can't wait for it.

Right now I spend every day in this swamp. Not a lot happens here.

Sometimes a colorful butterfly flutters by, or the wind blows wild-flower petals.

And I like colors so very much!

But when my MBDL comes, everything will change.

For the rest of the day, the animals told the bug about their adventures and had great fun.

When the sun set peace and quiet spread across the forest and wetlands. Fox and Boar fell asleep easily.

24

Look at how many of those blue flowers grow here. They are beautiful.

They are called forget-me-nots.

I will never forget them. Let's pick some for Mayfly. She will surely like them.

And these yellow ones?

It is balsam. It's a very sweet flower that loves to be picked.

Then we'll pick these flowers, too.

And these?

These are poppy heads. If you tap them, you can hear the poppy seeds rattle inside.

So the day went by.

Tiny Fox and Great Boar spent the day searching, picking flowers, and making plans for later.

They did not even notice that dusk had started to fall.

28

29

Suddenly everything turned dark. The wetlands were surrounded by absolute silence.

Dawn

Fox did not hear anything.
He did not understand anything.

He was running ahead.

The grasses on the wetlands were swaying
and breaking under Fox's paws. Dark water
was sloshing around threateningly.

Fox kept running. The shadow
of sadness was chasing him.
It was getting bigger.

The air thickened.

The harder it was to breathe, the stronger Fox's heart beat.

Fox was sitting on a cliff, looking at the river. Sad thoughts he had never had before kept passing through his head.

The longer he looked into the river's current, the more the darkness surrounded him.

Cloudy water was winding between the rocks and mosses.

Waterfalls hissed and growled over the rocky beds.

44

Night

The clouds were disappearing, and the sun came to the meadow.

48

Fox, this is not your fault.
She did not die because of you. Remember when we first met. You were angry at me because I wanted to eat all your apples.
You thought badly of me then. You thought I was greedy and unkind. But nothing bad happened to me, and then we became best friends.
Mayfly did not die because you were jealous. She was meant to live only one day.

Mayfly knew what would happen. She was waiting for this day.

We are the ones who don't understand it, since our life still goes on.

We should find her.

She can't lie there alone. We have to bid her farewell.

The animals found Mayfly and brought her to the forest edge, where they could hear the stream murmuring and smell the mosses.

Fox, I will always be with you.

Shall we go further?

Yes.

Early sketches of Mayfly, as well as a look at the early concept art for the front cover of this book. Can you draw a mayfly?

A few pages from the author's sketchbook. A sketchbook is a good place
to write down stories, draw pictures, and come up with new ideas.
Try starting your own sketchbook today!

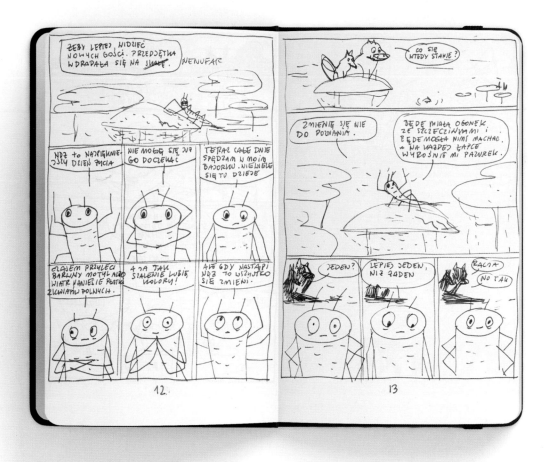

Early paintings from the pages of this book. Tiny Fox and Great Boar were so sad to lose their friend Mayfly, but they will remember her forever in their hearts.

Tiny Fox sitting peacefully in a calm meadow. Try to relax outside and enjoy all the sights, sounds, and smells that nature has to offer.

Berenika Kołomycka

Berenika Kołomycka is a comics author, sketch artist, sculptor, and graphic artist. She graduated from the Academy of Fine Arts in Warsaw and earned the Grand Prix for comics at the International Festival of Comics and Games in Łódź. Her works have been published in both Polish and foreign magazines, as well as in schoolbooks. She regularly conducts comic workshops for adults and children. The children's comic book series *Tiny Fox and Great Boar* is her first solo project. Outside of her work, she enjoys taking care of her cat, Mami, and her dog, Kuka.

Crank!

Christopher Crank (crank!) has lettered a bunch of books put out by Image, Dark Horse, Oni Press, Dynamite, and elsewhere. He also has a podcast with comic artist Mike Norton and members of Four Star Studios in Chicago (crankcast.com), and makes music (sonomorti.bandcamp.com). Catch him on Twitter: @ccrank and Instagram: ccrank